10
Things I Know About Kangaroos

Written by
Wendy Wax and Della Rowland

With Illustrations by
Thomas Payne

A CALICO BOOK
Published by Contemporary Books, Inc.
CHICAGO · NEW YORK

Library of Congress Cataloging-in-Publication Data

Wax, Wendy
    10 things I know about kangaroos / written by Wendy Wax and Della Rowland: illustrated by Thomas Payne.
      p.   cm.
    "A Calico book."
    Summary: A simple introduction to this Australian animal whose male members are called boomers, whose female members are called flyers, and whose babies are called joeys.
    ISBN 0-8092-4350-4
    1. Kangaroos—Juvenile literature.   [1. Kangaroos.]   I. Rowland, Della, II. Payne, Tom, ill.   III. Title.   IV. Title: Ten things I know about kangaroos.
OL737.M35R68   1989
599.2—dc19   88-37548
                                                                               CIP
                                                                               AC

All photos courtesy of Animals Animals/Earth Scenes. Fritz Prenzel: cover, pages 6-7, 20-21; Mickey Gibson: page 3; M. Austerman: page 4; J. C. Stevenson: page 4, OSF/A.G. Wells: page 4; David C. Fritts: pages 8-9, 10, 12, 15, 16; E. R. Degginger: page 19.

Copyright © 1989 by The Kipling Press
Text copyright © 1989 by Della Rowland and Wendy Wax
Illustrations copyright © 1989 by Thomas Payne
Designed by Kris Gonzalez
All rights reserved
Published by Contemporary Books, Inc.
180 North Michigan Avenue, Chicago, Illinois 60601
Manufactured in the United States of America
International Standard Book Number: 0-8092-4350-4

Published simultaneously in Canada by Beaverbooks, Ltd.
195 Allstate Parkway, Valleywood Business Park
Markham, Ontario L3R 4T8 Canada

10
Things I Know About Kangaroos

1

Kangaroos live only
in Australia and on nearby islands.

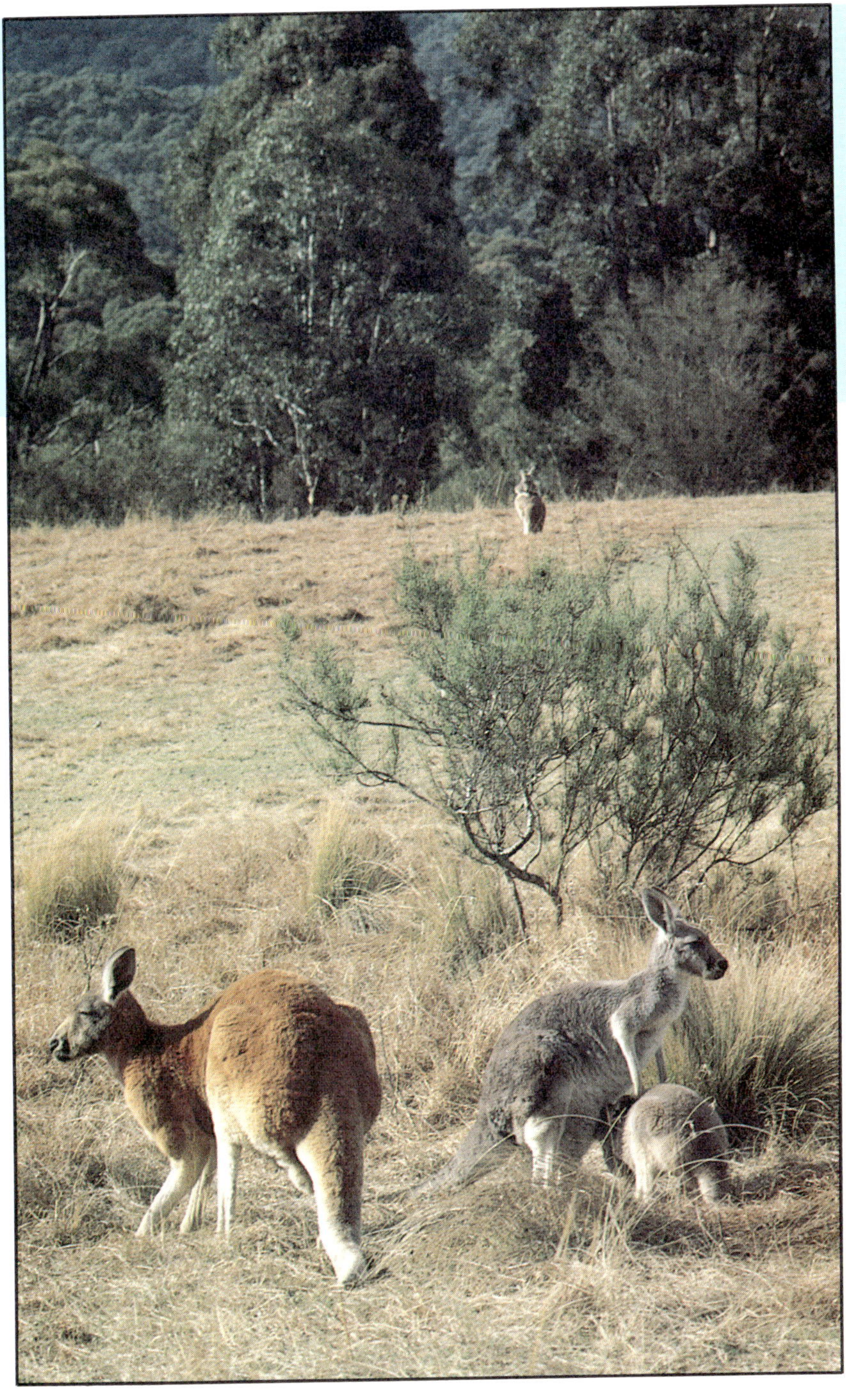

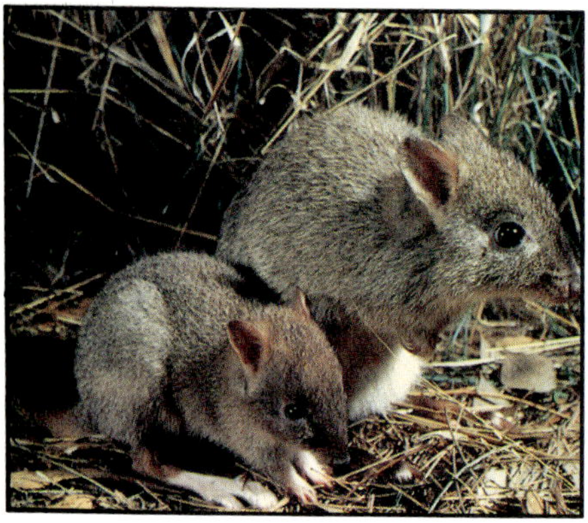

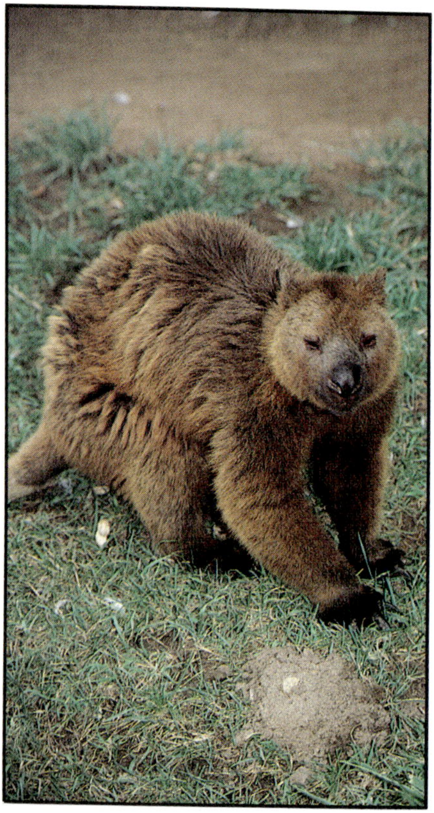

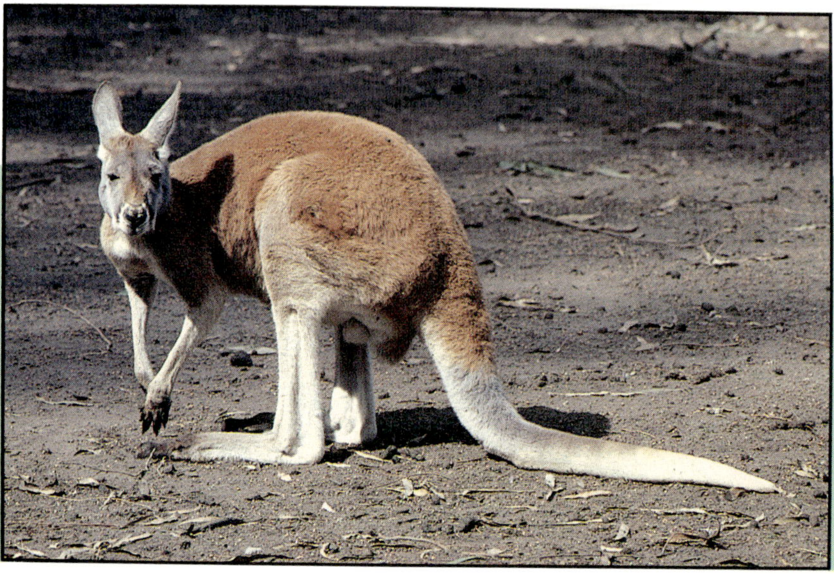

2 There are fifty different kinds of kangaroos. The smallest is only as big as a rabbit. The largest stands nearly seven feet tall.

A kangaroo's big feet and
long tail help it jump great distances.

3

The largest kangaroo can jump farther than any other animal on earth can— forty-four feet in one leap!

BOING!

4

5

Kangaroos like to
eat grass,
and they prefer to eat at night.

6

The male kangaroo is called
a boomer. The female kangaroo
is a doe. And a baby
kangaroo is a joey.

7

Boomers fight each other
when it's time to choose a mate.
They sit back on their
tails and scratch and kick.

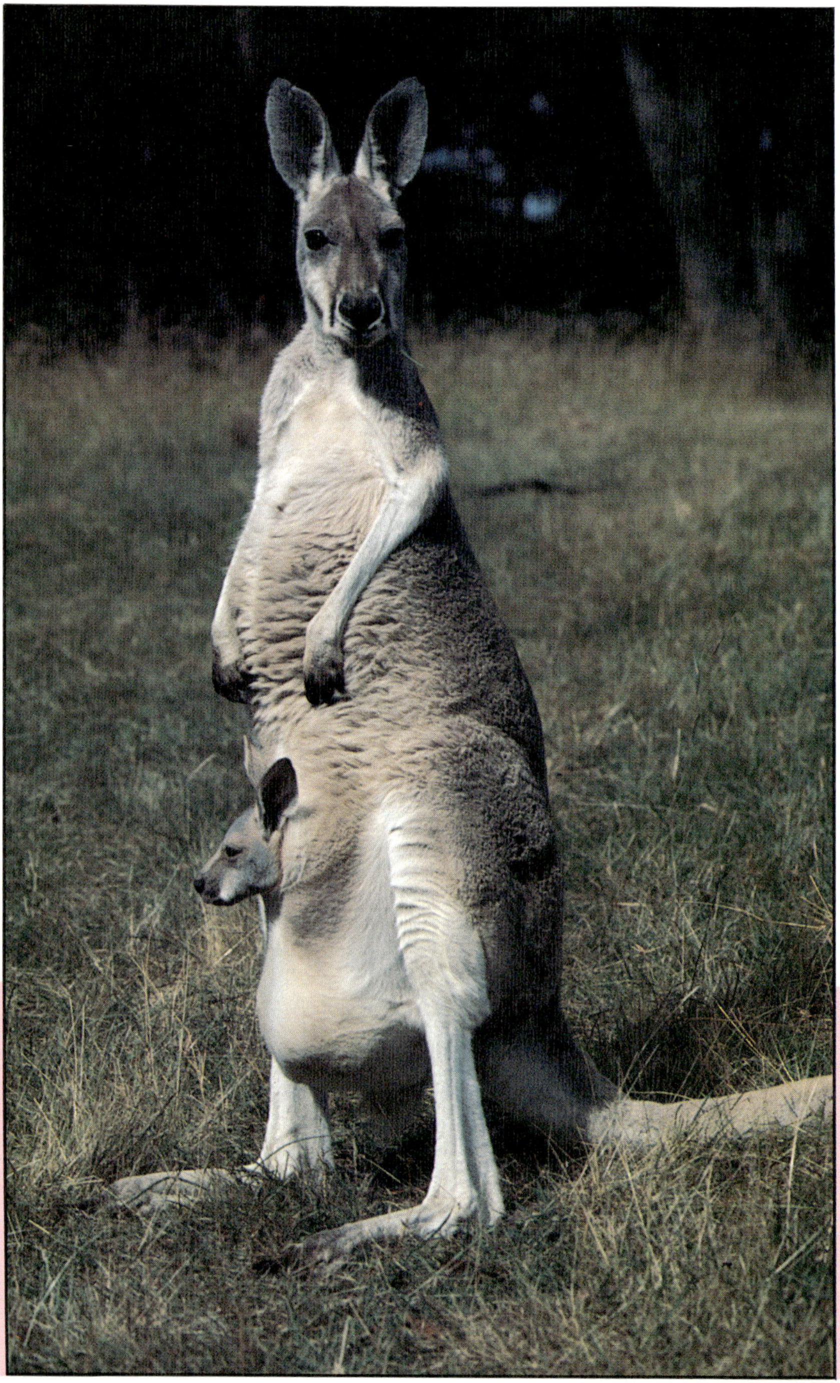

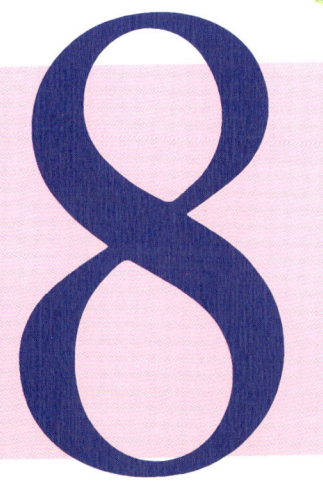

8 When a joey is born, it is as small as a lima bean. The doe carries it in her pouch, where it sucks milk and grows.

When the joey outgrows
the pouch, it can still stick
its head in to get milk.

WHOOPS!

9

Kangaroos live in groups called mobs.

10

BOING!